Thanks for Thanksgiving

by **Julie Markes**

illustrated by **Doris Barrette**

■ **HARPERCOLLINSPUBLISHERS**

Thanks for Thanksgiving
Text copyright © 2004 by Julie Markes
Illustrations copyright © 2004 by Doris Barrette
Manufactured in China by South China Printing Company Ltd.

www.harperchildrens.com

Library of Congress Cataloging-in-Publication Data
Markes, Julie.
Thanks for Thanksgiving / by Julie Markes ; illustrated by Doris Barrette.—
1st ed.
p.   cm.
Summary: At Thanksgiving time, children express their gratitude for people
and things in their lives.
ISBN 0-06-051096-X
[1. Thanksgiving Day—Fiction. 2. Gratitude—Fiction. 3. Stories in rhyme.]
I. Barrette, Doris, ill. II. Title.
PZ8.3.M391445 Th 2004   [E]—dc21   2002153420
CIP   AC

Typography by Stephanie Bart-Horvath
4   5   6   7   8   9   10
❖
First Edition

To my amazing mother, Diana,
for whom I am very thankful.
—J.M.

To my parents, Cécile and Gérald.
—D.B.

Thanks for Thanksgiving,
for turkey and pie.

Thank you for fall
and gold leaves floating by.

Thank you for music
and dancing and art.

Thank you for play dates,
for swings and for slides.

Thank you for hopscotch
and piggyback rides.

Thanks for sweet puppies
and soft, furry cats.

Thank you for dress-up,
red shoes and big hats.

Thanks for umbrellas,
for rain boots and puddles.

Thank you for Mommy
and warm, cozy cuddles.

Thank you for Daddy
and rides on a sled.

Thank you for kisses
and tucks into bed.

Thanks for the moon
and the stars up above,

But MOST of all, thanks for the family I love!

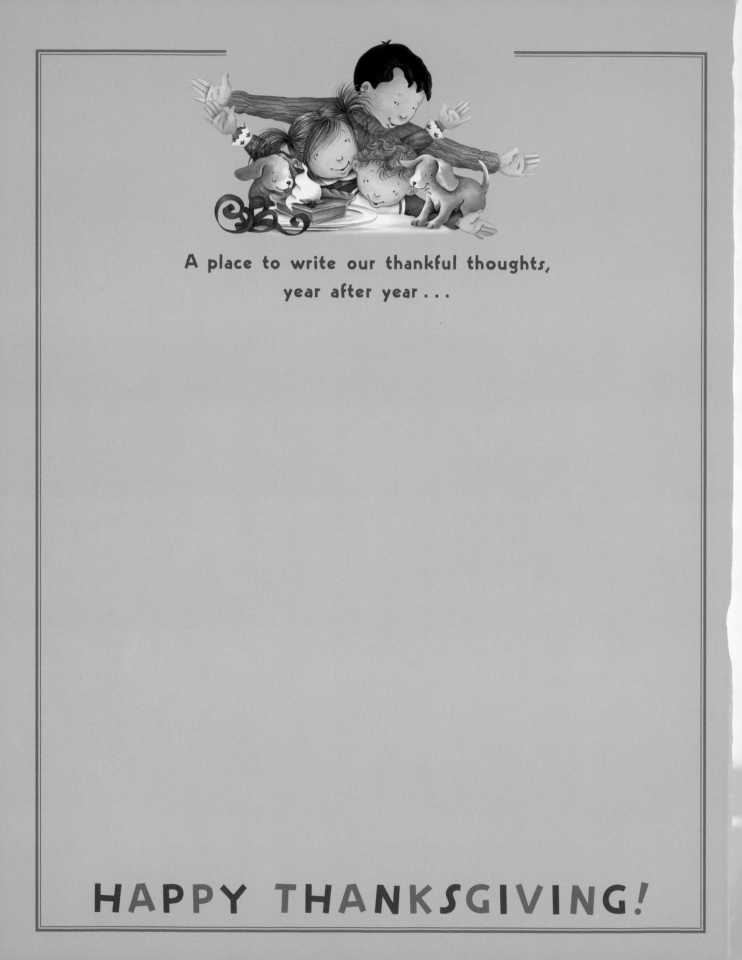

A place to write our thankful thoughts,
year after year . . .

HAPPY THANKSGIVING!